Kilkenny Libraries
KK519693

D0528476

A TEMPLAR BOOK

First published in the UK in 2018 by Templar Publishing,
an imprint of Kings Road Publishing, part of the Bonnier Publishing Group,
The Plaza, 535 King's Road, London, SW10 0SZ
www.bonnierpublishing.com

First published by Penguin Random House Australia Pty Ltd, 2017

1 3 5 7 9 10 8 6 4 2

ISBN 978-1-78741-235-4

This book was typeset in Eames Century Mode.
The illustrations were created in watercolour, pencil and digitally.

Printed in Malaysia

What's at the top?

Is it a hat?

Or a black-and-white cat?

Is it a dog?

Or a frog on a log?

It could be a boat…

Or a castle and moat?

An invisible man?

Or a door to Japan?

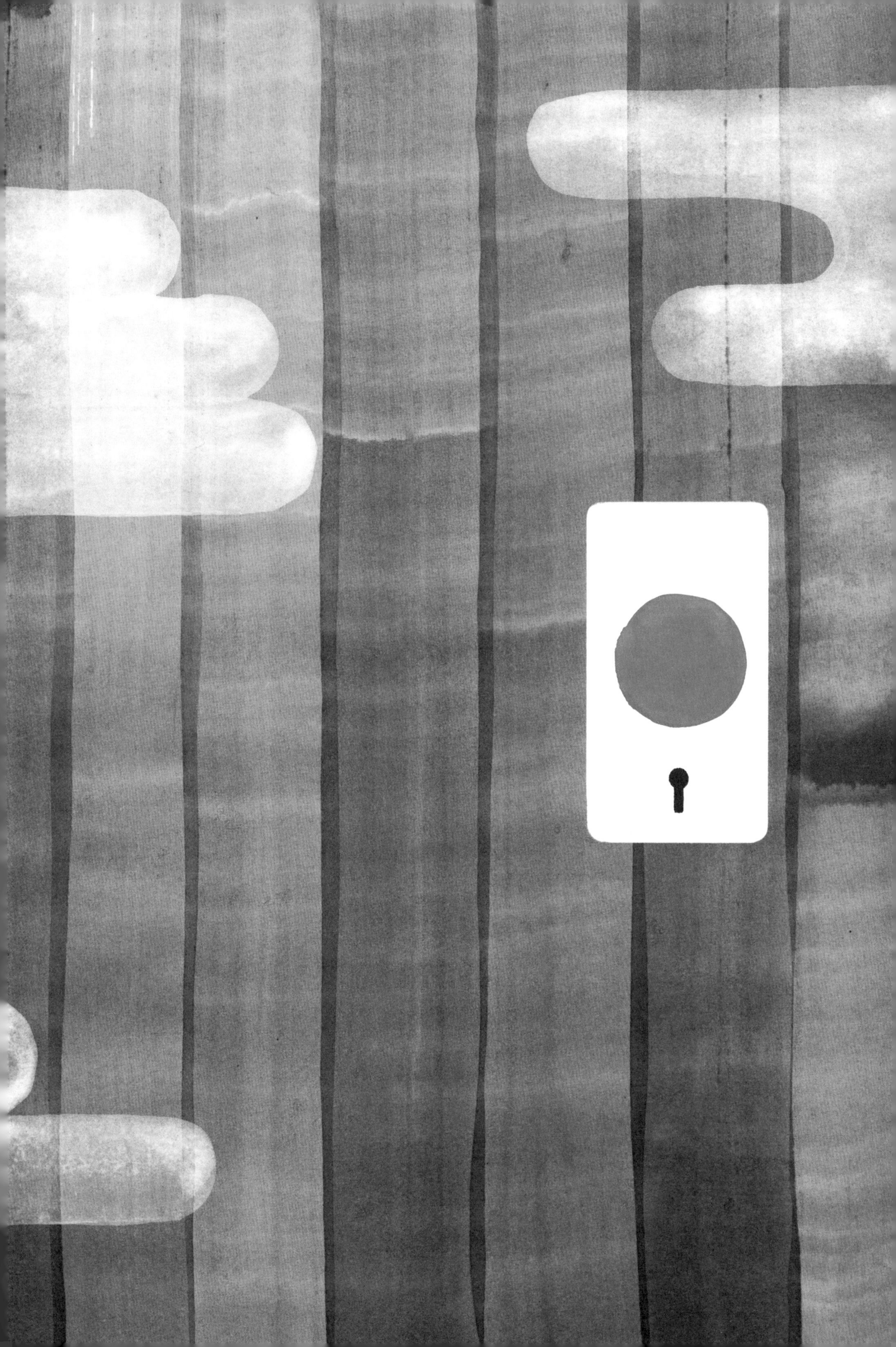

I hope it's not rain,
or a really fast train!

Or the end of a rope
down a very steep slope!

It could be the moon
or a yellow balloon…

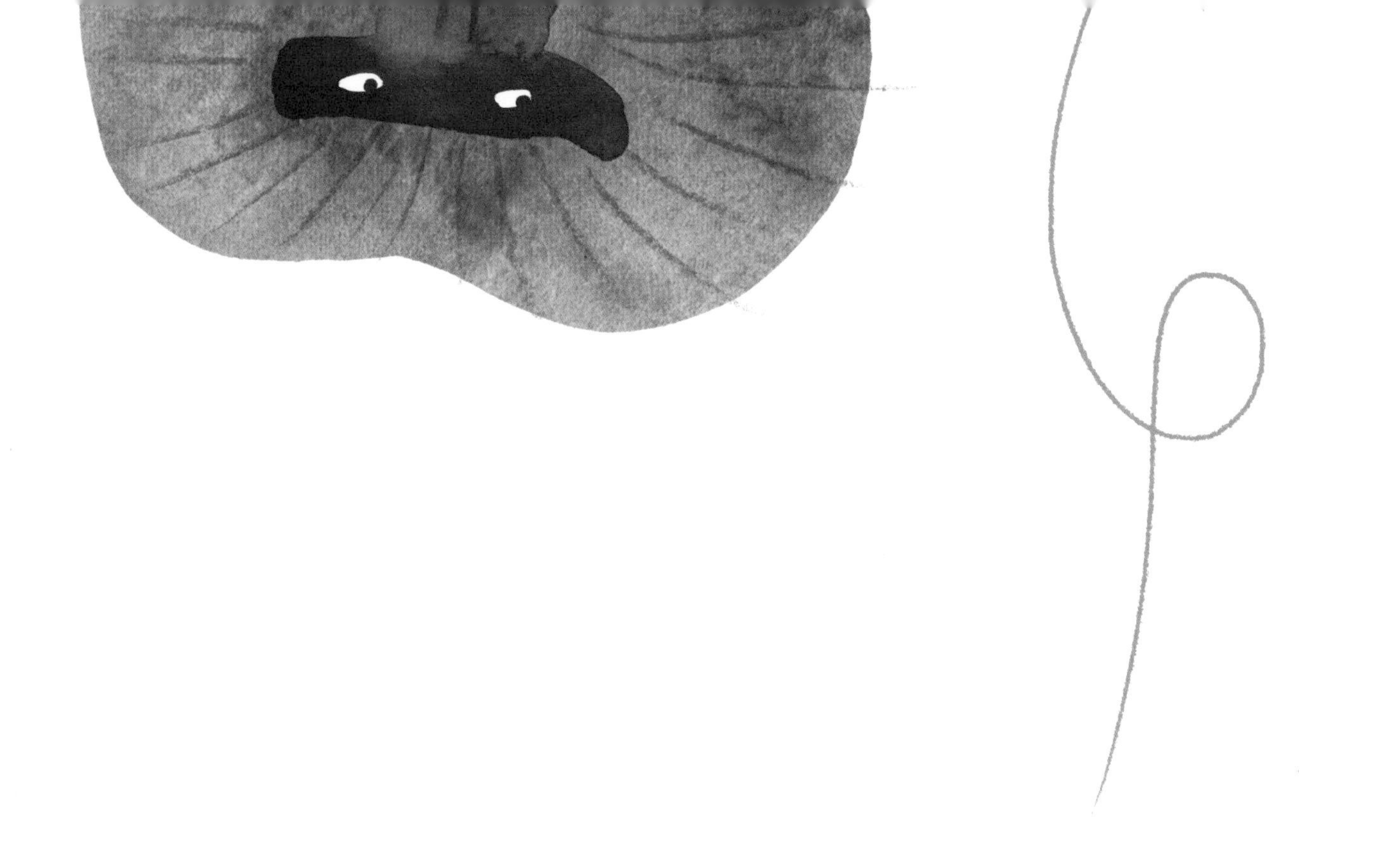

Is it safe to assume
that it's not a baboon?

NEWS

Maybe somebody tall
standing next to a wall,
or a giant giraffe
that thinks it's still small?

What about a hotel
that looks like a shell,
that's run by a snail
with the name of Miguel?

HOTEL

NO
PETS

Or…

…the string of a kite
on a meteorite
that's attached to a whale
who's delivering mail
to a moose in a suit
wearing boots made of fruit
while a sloth eating soup
parachutes through a hoop
for a group of iguanas
in purple pyjamas?

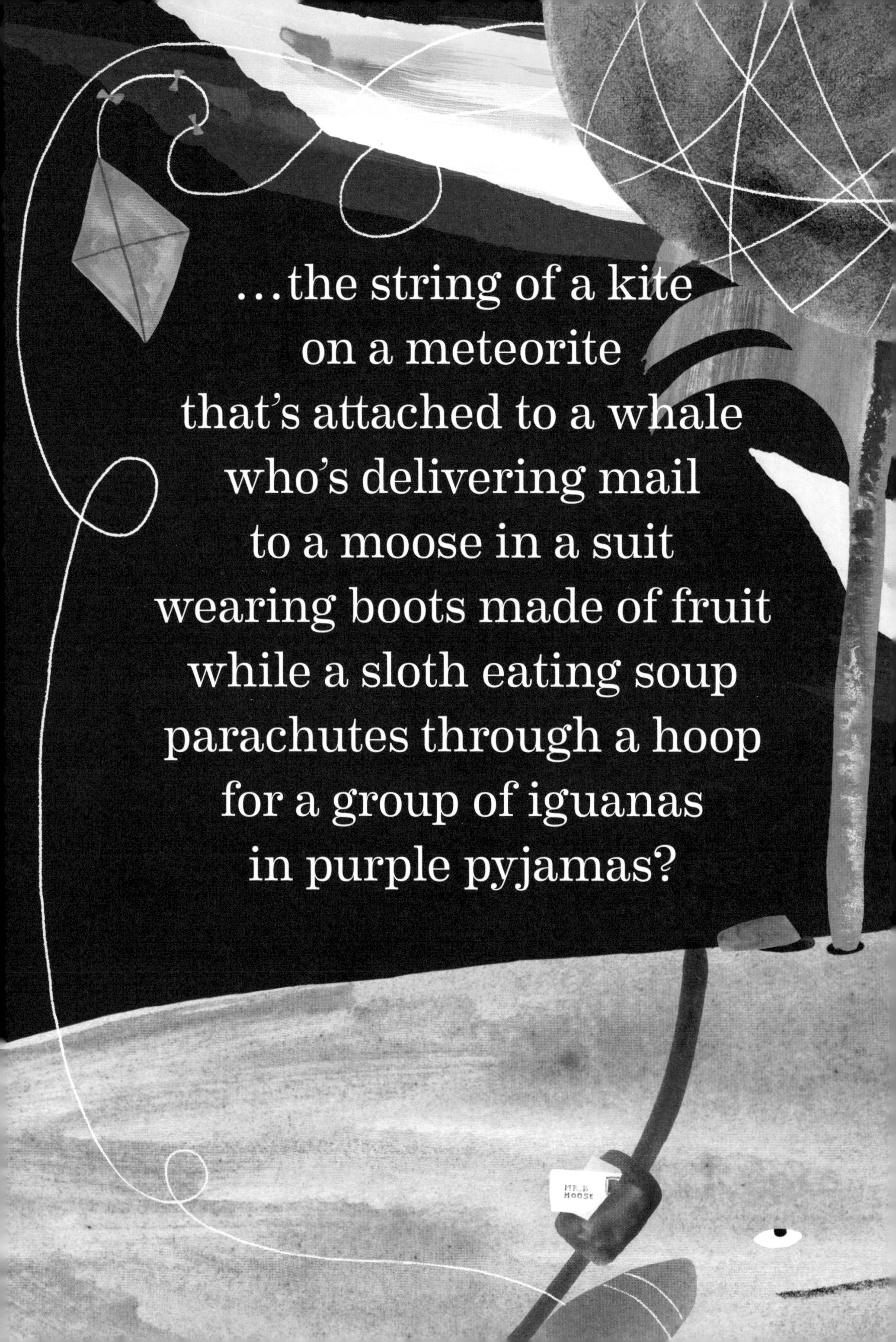

9
9
8
9
MR.
BRUCE
MOOSE

Whatever's up there,
it's sure to be high.

So it could be a bird...
or maybe just sky.

To be totally honest,
I'm not sure what's right…

I don't climb up ladders...
I'm not good with heights!

So I'll leave it here,
but before we stop,
perhaps *you* can tell me…

What's at the top?